www.mascotbooks.com

For more information, please contact:
Mascot Books
560 Herndon Parkway #120
Herndon, VA 20170
info@mascotbooks.com

CPSIA Code: PRT0913A
ISBN-10: 1620862867
ISBN-13: 9781620862865

Printed in the United States

THAT'S NOT OUR MASCOT?™
Truman is Our Mascot

MISSOURI®

by **Jason Wells and Jeff Wells**
illustrated by **Patrick Carlson**

That's not our mascot...

it's Big Red, the Arkansas Razorback.

Who's that playing in the
Marching Mizzou?

That's not our mascot...
it's Aubie, the Auburn Tiger.

That's not our mascot...
it's Albert, the Florida Gator.

Who's that batting in Taylor Stadium?

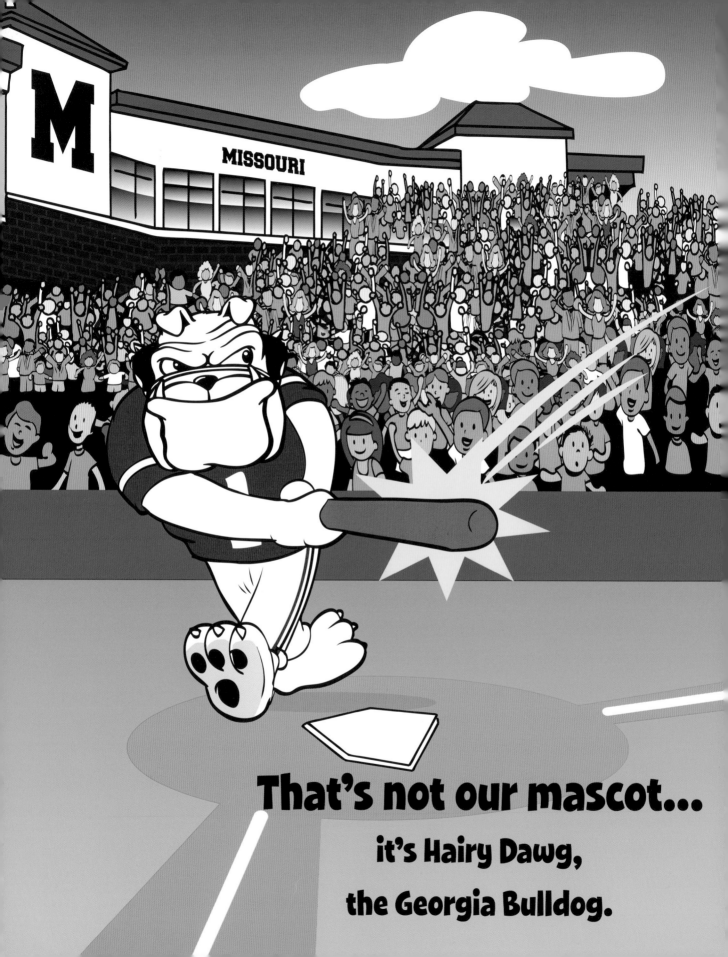

That's not our mascot...
it's Hairy Dawg,
the Georgia Bulldog.

Who's that running in the Tiger Walk?

That's not our mascot...
it's Scratch, the Kentucky Wildcat.

Who's that playing Big MO?

That's not our mascot...
it's Big Al, the Alabama Elephant.

That's not our mascot...
it's Bully, the Mississippi State Bulldog.

Who's that playing on Carnahan Quad?

That's not our mascot...

it's Mike, the LSU Tiger.

Who's that studying at Ellis Library?

Who's that sitting
on the rock "M"?

That's not our mascot...
it's Reveille from Texas A&M.

Who's that strolling by the Tiger Plaza?

That's not our mascot....
it's Mr. C, the Vanderbilt® Commodore.